SAINT FRANCIS AND THE CHRISTMAS DONKEY

Saint Francis and the Christmas Donkey

ROBERT BYRD

DUTTON CHILDREN'S BOOKS • NEW YORK

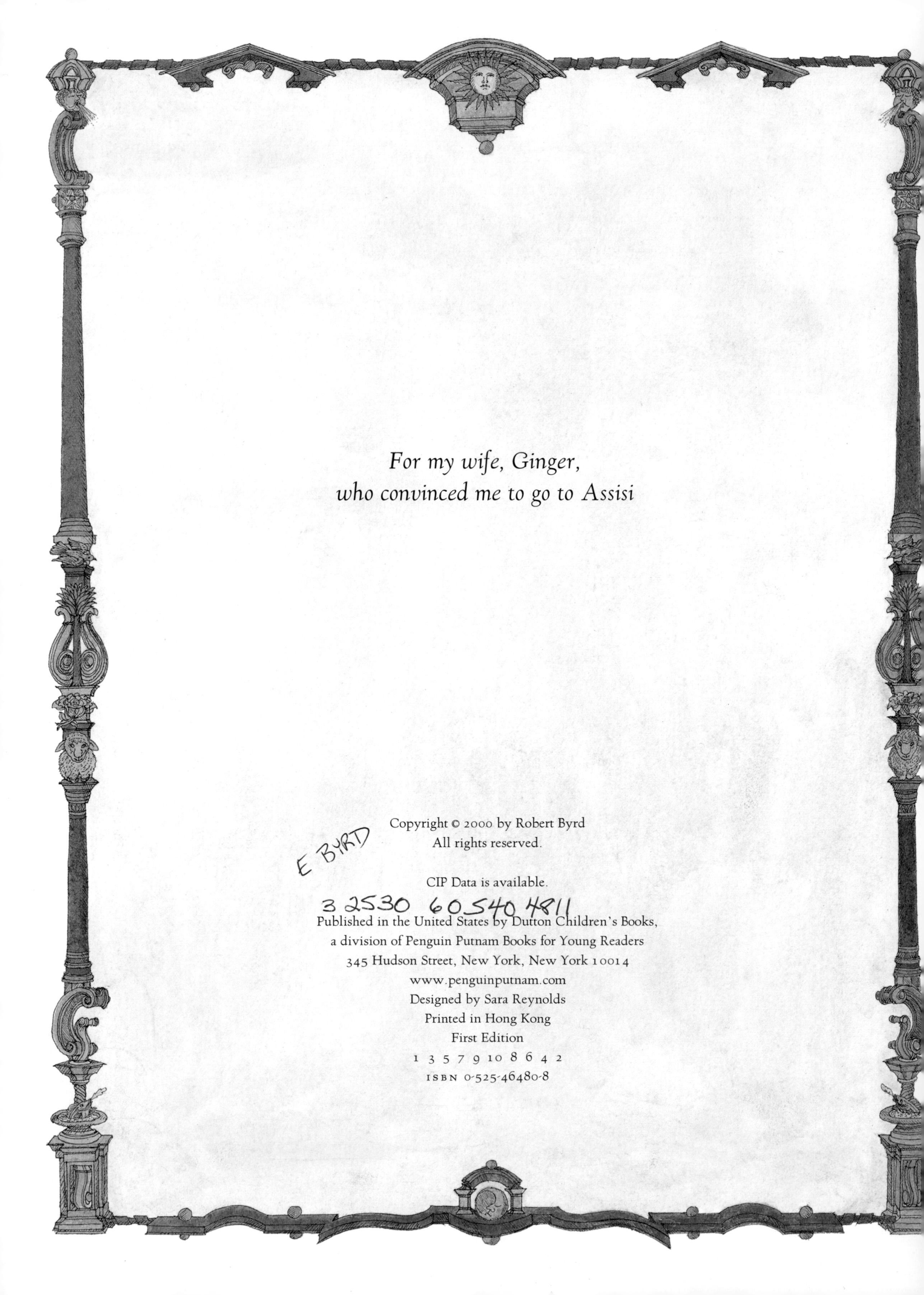

For my wife, Ginger,
who convinced me to go to Assisi

CIP Data is available.

Published in the United States by Dutton Children's Books,
a division of Penguin Putnam Books for Young Readers
345 Hudson Street, New York, New York 10014
www.penguinputnam.com
Designed by Sara Reynolds
Printed in Hong Kong
First Edition
1 3 5 7 9 10 8 6 4 2
ISBN 0-525-46480-8

Ye shall wait for me here upon the way
and I will go to preach unto my little sisters, the birds.

from I FIORETTI

{*The Little Flowers of Saint Francis of Assisi*}

Many years ago in Italy, there lived a gentle monk named Francis, who loved the beauty of all living things. He led a simple life with other monks in the hills and forests, where he marveled at the creatures around him.

Francis believed that nature and all its wonders were a gift from God. He vowed to do everything he could to take care of the birds, plants, animals, and trees.

The monks tended a garden where they grew their own food. Whenever Francis worked in the garden, the forest animals came and sat peacefully nearby, watching him. When he spoke to them, they understood his words.

He called them his "little brothers" and reminded them how precious they all were, from the tiniest mouse to the powerful great gray wolf.

Francis talked to the birds about their marvelous gifts of flight and song. He called them his "little sisters," and their voices filled the air with music. Francis knew that people should respect and honor all living things. He was the first person of his time to teach others that animals, too, were God's creatures and should be treated with kindness.

Wherever Francis went, the birds and animals followed him. Walking in a dark forest late one winter's day, he heard a loud, sad, braying noise and came upon a small donkey.

"My friend," said Francis, "why do you call out in such an unhappy voice?"

"You would cry out yourself," said the donkey, "if your work was as hard as mine. Ever since the beginning of time, we donkeys have carried heavy loads on our small backs, and people and animals have made fun of the way we sound.

"This does not seem fair," the donkey said to Francis. "Can you tell me why we have always been treated this way?"

"Perhaps I may be able to," answered Francis. "Some things take time to understand, and some things we may never know. But I believe the tale of the donkey is a very special one, with a wonderful ending. Sit down and I will tell it to you."

The donkey was amazed to hear this. He sat down eagerly, filled with curiosity, as Francis began his story.

In the beginning, when God created the animals, He made the smallest ones first.

He made the worm, the snail, the crab, and the shrew.

Then He made creatures that were a little bigger. He made the mouse, the frog, the rabbit, and the mole.

And then some a little bigger than that—the tortoise, the fox, the dog, and the cat.

And next some bigger still—the goat, the aardvark, the hyena, and the monkey.

He made hundreds of others, and He delighted in the way they crawled, swam, hopped, walked, and ran.

He made even larger animals, too—the cow, the horse, and the hippopotamus,

the bear, the buffalo, and the deer,

the great apes, and many, many more. Hundreds and thousands more.

God was especially pleased with the donkey, who was very spirited and full of life. Thrilled by everything he saw, the donkey jumped and kicked his heels and sang out in a most extraordinarily beautiful voice.

One day he happened to see his reflection in a pond.

Why, I am the most handsome animal there is, the donkey thought, admiring his delicate ears and tiny tail. He pranced around with his nose in the air and began to have quite a high opinion of himself.

Meanwhile, God was not finished using His great imagination. He began to create animals of astounding shapes and sizes.

He made the snake, with no arms or legs. It slithered along the ground. When the donkey saw this, he laughed out loud.

God made the giraffe, with a neck so long that its head stuck up above the tops of the trees.

"How ridiculous," scoffed the donkey. "What a silly-looking thing."

God made a camel with one hump. But even God was not sure this worked. So he tried a camel with two humps.

At this, the arrogant donkey exclaimed:

"Preposterous! First with one hump, then with two—
Maybe three or four will do!"

"Your behavior is quite inappropriate," roared the lion.

"You are ignorant and most unwise," snarled the tiger.

"You are tiresome, rude, and simpleminded," growled the leopard.

When God made the elephant, the donkey was beside himself.

"What silly creature have we here—
  So wrinkled, big, and round,
  With two enormous, floppy ears
  And a nose that reaches the ground!"

This was finally too much for the rest of the animals. They gathered around the donkey.

"Fool!" shouted the monkeys. They grabbed the donkey's ears and pulled.

"Hee-haw, hee-haw!" bawled the donkey. "Hee-haw! Hee-haw!" The donkey had never cried before and was surprised by the harsh sound of his voice. "Hee-haw, hee-haw!" This raucous noise was the only sound he could make. He tried to run away, but the monkeys held tight.

"Hee-haw, hee-haw!" cried the donkey more loudly, but the monkeys would not let go, and the donkey's ears began to stretch. The more the monkeys pulled, the louder the donkey brayed—and the longer his poor ears grew!

A chimpanzee tugged at the donkey's tiny tail, and it, too, began to stretch.

The donkey's cries became so loud, and such a commotion arose, that finally in a great booming voice, God himself called out, "Stop! Stop all this foolishness at once!"

God was furious. He said to the donkey, "You silly little beast. I have shown you favor, and how do you act? Why, you dare to laugh at the creatures I have made. Because of this, you shall always laugh, but your laugh will be an ugly sound. And when my creatures hear your loud, ridiculous 'Hee-haw! Hee-haw!' they all will laugh at you. And you shall keep those long, clumsy ears. Your tail will stay as scrawny and scraggly as a rope. You will always do the hardest work, carrying heavy loads for the rest of your days, wherever you go."

So you see," said Francis, "how those things became the lot of the poor donkey."

"That does not seem like such a good story to me," said the donkey, disappointed. "Where is the part you said was very special? The part with a wonderful ending?"

"Now just be patient," Francis said. "I have only told you the beginning of the story. Let me tell you the rest."

So Francis continued his tale.

The donkey went to work in the ancient world. In the pharaohs' Egypt, donkeys carried food and supplies to the men who built the mighty temples and pyramids.

Donkeys carried cotton, precious stones, ivory, and bolts of cloth and silk for the merchants in the bustling cities of Babylon, Tyre, and Byzantium.

And in ancient Rome, going to and from the busy markets, donkeys carried great baskets filled with olive oil, wine, fruit, vegetables, and grain.

Donkeys also lived in ancient Palestine. There, in a town called Nazareth, in the land of Galilee, one donkey worked for a carpenter named Joseph. A good man, Joseph treated the donkey with kindness.

Mary was Joseph's wife, and she was going to have a child.

The emperor of Rome, Caesar Augustus, ruled over Palestine. About this time, he gave orders that everyone in the land must go to the city of their ancestors. The emperor wanted to make a census, or a counting of all the people.

Joseph and Mary set out for the city of David, called Bethlehem, because their families had been born there. The journey from Nazareth would take several days and nights. Knowing Mary tired easily, Joseph decided the donkey should carry her.

They had to travel through steep, rugged mountains. Up and down they went, the donkey choosing his steps carefully on the rocky path. As he struggled on, Mary's weight seemed to grow heavier and heavier. Several times the donkey stumbled, but he did not fall.

They came to a vast, burning desert. The donkey grew weak as he pushed on through the hot sand. He was thirsty and his legs ached. Soon it did not seem possible that he could take one more step, yet he did not give up.

Instead, he thought of Mary on his back with her unborn child. Summoning all of the strength left in his little body, he brought her safely to Bethlehem.

It was late in the day when they arrived. The city was crowded with travelers, and all the inns were full.

The only place they could find room was in a stable. But they were so tired and had come such a long way, they were grateful for any shelter at all.

And that night, the donkey was there in the stable, beneath a cold, clear, star-filled sky, when Mary gave birth to Jesus.

Angels brought tidings of the birth to shepherds keeping watch over their flocks nearby. The shepherds came with their sheep to see the child. The donkey too looked on. His warm breath comforted the baby, who lay in a manger on a bed of hay.

Guided by a star in the east, three wise kings came to worship the newborn babe. They brought gifts of gold, frankincense, and myrrh—their most prized treasures. But these gifts were nothing compared with the love, devotion, and courage of the little donkey in the stable.

Francis paused for a moment, and the donkey spoke up in worry. "But the little donkey in the stable had no gift to give," he said sadly.

"Well," said Francis, "surely you can see that by carrying Mary and the baby Jesus, the Christmas donkey had truly given the most wonderful gift of all."

The little donkey knelt by the manger, watching the baby Jesus, Mary and Joseph, the angels, and the shepherds. He felt the gentleness of the other animals.

And in his own heart, in his very own way, the donkey knew what he had done, and he was happy.

Francis had finished his story. It was evening now. Snow had begun to fall. He took the donkey's head tenderly in his hands, and together they walked out of the woods.

When they emerged from the forest, they stopped and looked up into the vast sky. The silence of the cold winter's eve surrounded them. Through the softly falling snow, Francis and the donkey could see one brilliant star shining clearly in the peaceful night.

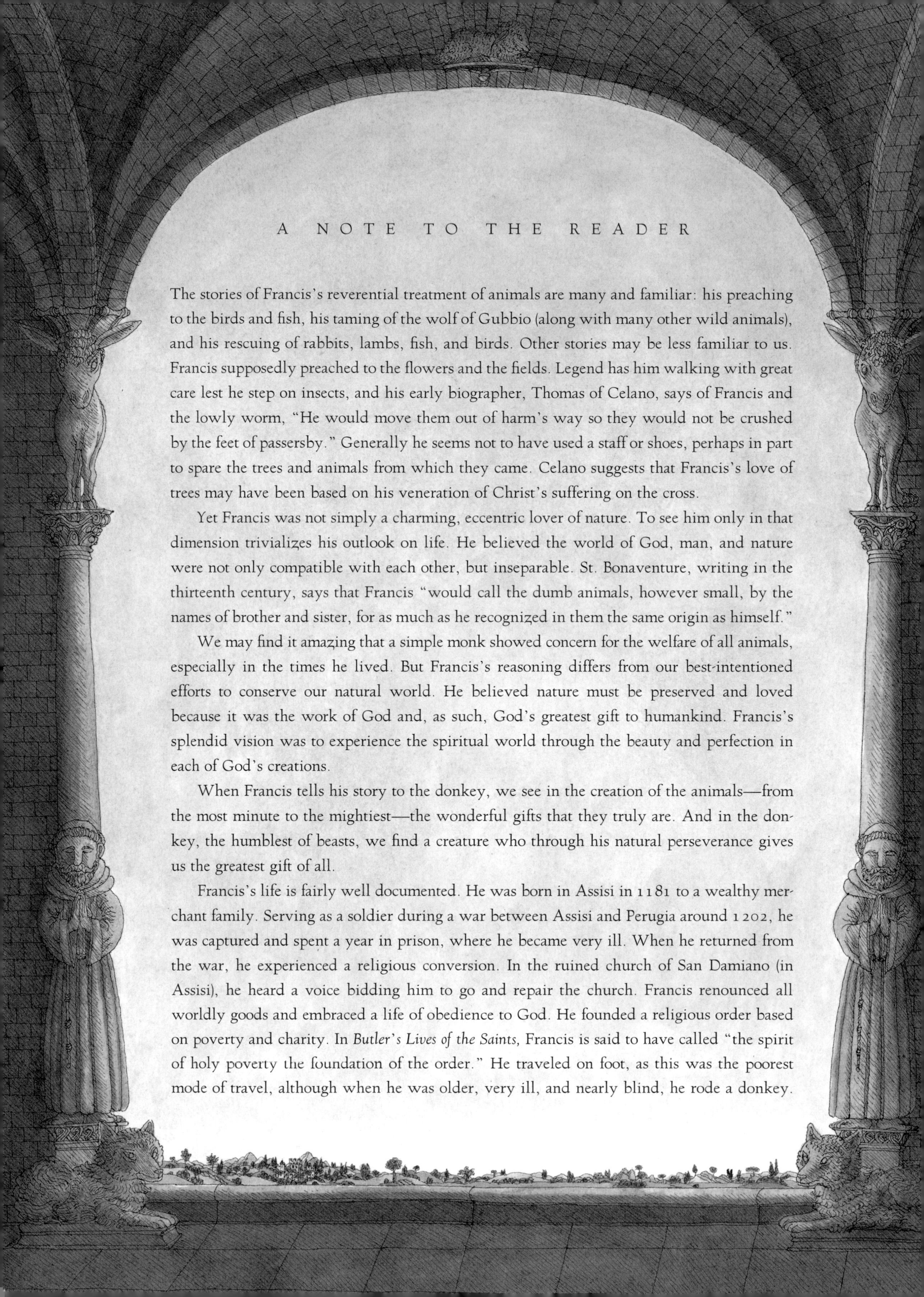

A NOTE TO THE READER

The stories of Francis's reverential treatment of animals are many and familiar: his preaching to the birds and fish, his taming of the wolf of Gubbio (along with many other wild animals), and his rescuing of rabbits, lambs, fish, and birds. Other stories may be less familiar to us. Francis supposedly preached to the flowers and the fields. Legend has him walking with great care lest he step on insects, and his early biographer, Thomas of Celano, says of Francis and the lowly worm, "He would move them out of harm's way so they would not be crushed by the feet of passersby." Generally he seems not to have used a staff or shoes, perhaps in part to spare the trees and animals from which they came. Celano suggests that Francis's love of trees may have been based on his veneration of Christ's suffering on the cross.

Yet Francis was not simply a charming, eccentric lover of nature. To see him only in that dimension trivializes his outlook on life. He believed the world of God, man, and nature were not only compatible with each other, but inseparable. St. Bonaventure, writing in the thirteenth century, says that Francis "would call the dumb animals, however small, by the names of brother and sister, for as much as he recognized in them the same origin as himself."

We may find it amazing that a simple monk showed concern for the welfare of all animals, especially in the times he lived. But Francis's reasoning differs from our best-intentioned efforts to conserve our natural world. He believed nature must be preserved and loved because it was the work of God and, as such, God's greatest gift to humankind. Francis's splendid vision was to experience the spiritual world through the beauty and perfection in each of God's creations.

When Francis tells his story to the donkey, we see in the creation of the animals—from the most minute to the mightiest—the wonderful gifts that they truly are. And in the donkey, the humblest of beasts, we find a creature who through his natural perseverance gives us the greatest gift of all.

Francis's life is fairly well documented. He was born in Assisi in 1181 to a wealthy merchant family. Serving as a soldier during a war between Assisi and Perugia around 1202, he was captured and spent a year in prison, where he became very ill. When he returned from the war, he experienced a religious conversion. In the ruined church of San Damiano (in Assisi), he heard a voice bidding him to go and repair the church. Francis renounced all worldly goods and embraced a life of obedience to God. He founded a religious order based on poverty and charity. In *Butler's Lives of the Saints,* Francis is said to have called "the spirit of holy poverty the foundation of the order." He traveled on foot, as this was the poorest mode of travel, although when he was older, very ill, and nearly blind, he rode a donkey.

Francis believed that by living a life of true poverty, as Christ had lived, and by loving this poverty, he could achieve the state of the most intense love of God.

His charismatic personality drew many followers to the hills and woods above Assisi. He visited the Holy Land in 1219 and died in Assisi in 1226. The Vatican canonized him in 1228; in 1979, it declared him the patron saint of ecology.

In 1223, in Greccio, Francis staged a re-creation of the Nativity scene with real children and animals, including a donkey. Shepherds sleeping in the fields with their sheep had reminded him of the first Christmas. The legend of the donkey's breath warming the Babe is mentioned by Thomas of Celano. Celano also suggests that a lullaby sung to the baby Jesus by Francis and the people of the Greccio crèche may have been the first Christmas carol. He states: "The brethren sang, yielding due praise to the Lord, and all that night sounded with jubilation."

Francis tried to have a law passed by the Holy Roman Emperor that would require people to give extra food to their animals on Christmas day and to scatter seed by the roadsides to feed his beloved birds.

The Gospels give no specific setting for the Nativity. I have chosen to set it in a stable, following the Italian or Western European style, as opposed to a cave, which is the Byzantine or earlier version. I have depicted a manger made of stone as was used in ancient Palestine, in contrast to the wooden versions seen in most European art. The donkey and the ox almost invariably appear in Western Nativity painting. They sometimes even kneel before the Child.

The donkey appears in three major episodes in Jesus' life: first in the Nativity story; then carrying Mary and Jesus in the flight into Egypt; and finally with Jesus entering Jerusalem on Palm Sunday, riding a young ass. Folklore tells us that Jesus, in gratitude for the donkey's warm breath in the cold manger, marked his back with a cross of dark hair. By that mark, the donkey's descendant could be chosen to carry Christ into Jerusalem on Palm Sunday.

The journey of Mary and Joseph to Bethlehem was about eighty miles. By donkey, the trip certainly would have taken several days.

The many retellings and variations of the Christmas story give us much to consider, as do the numerous Franciscan tales we so cherish. It is my sincere belief that the nature stories of Saint Francis, which have delighted us for ages, are not simply myths about an isolated mystic but reveal a vital, enthusiastic, and communal member of society—a man whose love of God and the natural world were overriding passions. I hope the story I have chosen gives a small glimpse into the life of this most beloved of men and the world in which he lived.

ROBERT BYRD, *February 2000*

ANNOTATED BIBLIOGRAPHY

Armstrong, Edward A. *Saint Francis: Nature Mystic*. Berkeley: University of California Press, 1973. Describes authoritatively the natural world Francis lived in and the various Franciscan nature legends familiar and unfamiliar, including their many discrepancies.

Arnold, T. W., trans. *The Little Flowers of St. Francis of Assisi*. London: Chatto and Windus, 1908. An anonymous fourteenth-century compilation, translated from the Italian, that gives accounts from Francis's life, such as the celebrated description of him preaching to the birds.

Gregori, Mina. *Paintings in the Uffizi and Pitti Galleries*. Boston: Little, Brown & Co., 1994. This lavish collection of art provides images by the thirteenth-century Italian masters, such as Giotto, Taddeo Gaddi, and the Master of the St. Francis paintings in the Bardi Chapel, many of which served as sources for the Italian architecture, landscapes, and Nativity scenes in this book.

Hartt, Frederick. *History of Italian Renaissance Art*. 3rd ed. Englewood Cliffs, N.J.: Prentice Hall, 1987. This volume contains many paintings of Francis and his medieval world, from the first known image of him in 1235 by Berlinghieri to Giotto and his school in the late Middle Ages, the Bellini family in the fifteenth century, and Giorgione in the early sixteenth.

Ives, C. F. *Picturesque Ideas on the Flight into Egypt*. New York: George Braziller, Inc., 1972. A series of masterful etchings by Giovanni Domenico Tiepolo depicting the flight into Egypt, which proved especially useful for my pictures of the journey to Bethlehem.

Maier, Paul. *First Christmas, the True and Unfamiliar Story*. New York: Harper & Row, 1971. Served as my primary reference, clearly explaining the ancient Roman and Palestinian world as it was in the time of Jesus' birth.

Thurston, Herbert J. and Donald Attwater, eds. *Butler's Lives of the Saints*. Vol. 4. Westminster, Md.: Christian Classics, 1990. Gives a concise account of Francis's views on chastity, humility, obedience, and poverty, all of which were central to his faith.

Untermeyer, Louis. *The Donkey of God and Other Stories*. New York: Harcourt Brace & Co., 1932. Untermeyer's short story "The Donkey of God" suggested to me the dialogue between Francis and the donkey.

The Gospels of Matthew and Luke were instrumental in furnishing information for both the Nativity text and the pictures.

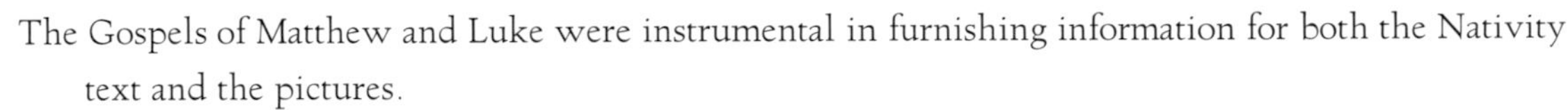